PRAISE FO

The standout winner in our ... ry Tale Competition, Sofia Ashdown's *Trolled* turns elements of Norse mythology and fairy tale into a hard-hitting YA tale that taps into very contemporary issues. The words and archetypes persist, being made relevant for a modern readership. Playing with the double meanings, Sofia's cleverness is to give an echo of the older meanings to her dark, sharply contemporary story.

— EDITOR OF WRITING MAGAZINE

URBAN FAIRY TALES

A SHORT STORY COLLECTION

S. A. ASHDOWN

BROOKER
PRESS
LTD

CONTENTS

"I am not free while any woman is unfree, even when her shackles are very different from my own."

— AUDRE LORDE

1

TROLLED

'Found mauled under the bridge by the glacier, along with two goats. An evening hike gone terribly wrong or another suicide?'

Helga glanced at her wolfhound, Fenrir, and leaned over to switch off the radio as her father pushed open the door, snow dusting the carpet. He heaved the woodpile to the basket and poked at the fire. 'Leave it on, snowflake.'

Helga, fourteen and blonde, feigned the vacant look expected of her. 'Sure,' she said. Fenrir nuzzled her hand as she gazed out over the frozen turquoise lake. She pulled it away as if she could still feel the blood on his nose. Last night, oh last night.

It wasn't him, she thought.

No one would believe her.

'Didn't you know her?'

'What?' Helga swallowed.

'The girl they found. She went to your school.'

'This is Olden; everyone goes to my school.' Helga pretended to stretch, yawned. Fenrir followed her to her small bedroom. Reds, pinks, splattered her wallpaper and bed. She grabbed her laptop and crawled onto the bed. A page online, a virtual memorial for Anette.

The trolls had taken over already: *fat goat got what she deserved... not talking about the animals*. Angry fingers scrunched over the keyboard. Should she comment? Nice words to drown out the anonymous bullies. No, not Helga. She let taps turn to virtual punches. *Tell us who you are, coward. Tell us your name. You have no power when we find out who you are!*

Out came the daggers, counter insults. *Bloody trolls, I'll find you!*

It did no good.

It was cold outside, even under Helga's puffy jacket and boots, but that didn't stop her deft descent downhill on skis. Fenrir followed, nose to the ground. Every local knew where the bridge in Olden was. Round the lake, hike a little to the glacier. Helga tried not to think of Anette, the fourth victim in as many months, coming by this route, even though she must have. Old bits of police tape tangled in the wilderness like tumbleweed. *Four teens dead,* she thought. The goats though, that was new. She glanced at Fenrir.

Helga recognised the policewoman standing under the bridge. Nothing to see now of course except dark patches of snow where the ground had been bruised with blood. 'Freya,' Helga whispered, out of shock. She hadn't intended to catch Freya's attention, just to look and leave.

Freya immediately clocked Fenrir. Helga wished she hadn't come. Of course it was stupid. 'Do you come up here often, with that hound?'

'First time,' she said. *Lie.*

'You should go home. This is a potential crime scene.' Freya nodded to the tape.

'Okay.' Helga couldn't think of anything better to say. She couldn't take her eyes of those dark splotches. Evening shadows hung like a shroud over the tree-line as Helga strapped her skis back on and started downhill.

Then she saw it. The lake house. The... *ogre*. He looked like that to her anyway, a round blob in a red jacket, broken teeth that smiled at her. A wrong smile. She hadn't even noticed the cabin this time on the way up; she'd been watching the path ahead, thinking.

The man said nothing until she'd almost passed. Then he laughed. Helga's anger bubbled up. 'What's so funny?'

'Good view of the bridge from here.'

Fenrir growled. Helga pulled her jacket in. In her periphery, she saw the man doing something with his hands. Wrapping corn. Glancing back, she counted the line-up of little scarecrows somehow staked into the frozen ground, dripping icicles. He was working on the fourth. Helga shivered and pressed on. In the distance, she spotted her father standing on their front porch, chewing his lip like he always did when he was worried.

'Where have you been? There's something out there, snowflake. Be careful.'

'Fenrir needed a walk. I'm fine.' Helga wanted to tell him about the ogre but next to the warmth of the wood burner, it seemed like a silly superstition. Father bought her a hot chocolate just as someone slammed the knocker on the front door.

Freya stood outside with Helga's cousin, Mikael, who had joined the *politi* last year. Low murmurs passed between Helga's father and Freya.

'They need to take Fenrir for some tests, snowflake.'

Helga jumped up from the carpet. 'No! He didn't do anything!'

Freya held up her hands and come inside slowly, like Helga was the rabid dog. 'We need to check his claws for DNA, just to rule him out. He's a big dog.'

'He didn't kill Anette.'

'No one is saying that.'

Father shackled Fenrir. Helga couldn't watch as he left with Freya, leaving Mikael to stay behind. 'He didn't do it.'

'I told Freya he's harmless. But people want answers.'

Helga stormed into her room. Mikael didn't bother to knock. 'Want to make a fort like we used to?'

'I'm not a kid anymore. But you might as well see something.' Helga sat on the bed and opened her laptop, bringing up Anette's memorial page. It didn't take long for Mikael to find the slurs.

'What about the other victims. Are their pages like this too?'

Helga nodded. 'Anette's is the worst. How can people be so cruel?'

'Interesting.'

'What?'

Mikael shrugged. 'That they've all been trolled.'

Helga shot Mikael an accusing stare. 'Shouldn't you and Freya be doing something about this? Instead of harassing Fenrir?'

'Trolls are nothing new.'

'But...' Helga thought about Anette, her strange behaviour before she vanished. Distant. Then jubilant. Helga never considered those hugs were a goodbye. 'What if the victims were bullied into it?'

Mikael's cheeks paled. 'Could be a suicide pact.'

'Anette didn't hang out with the others. And why jump months apart?' Helga jumped up, excited, then sat back down, yanking the laptop away from Mikael. 'We've had the same passwords since we owned computers,' she said. 'We used to hack each other's email and leave funny messages.'

They didn't find any funny messages this time. Just abuse. Reams and reams of abuse. Pictures too; dissected dolls, Photoshopped images of Anette, morphing the pretty girl into some kind of monster.

'Oh God.'

'Helga, you're onto something. This isn't right.' He started making phone calls while Helga plunged though Anette's inbox but after a while it became too much.

'Bring up another window, Helga.' Mikael rattled off email

addresses, password combinations given by the last victim's parents. It felt like forever. At last, a hit.

'It's exactly the same, just the images are different.' She checked Anette's inbox again, and found a deleted email that made her heave. She grasped Mikael's elbow as he hung up the phone.

'Look,' she said, pointing at the three scarecrows staked into the ground, a spot marked out in the snow. Written underneath: *Jump from the bridge, otherwise you're next. Do it tonight*. 'That's Anette's last email.'

The ogre. It must be him. 'Mikael, I think I know who the troll is.'

Mikael tried to radio Freya as Helga recounted her journey home. 'Freya's not answering. Must have left the radio in the jeep.'

'We need to do something.'

'I need a permit to search the cabin.'

Helga smiled. 'Not if you're rescuing me.'

'No way – Helga!' But she'd already grabbed her jacket and tugged on her snow boots. He chased her onto the porch and caught her. 'Damn, left my radio on the bed.'

Helga took her chance and ran through the snow, into the darkness. She fell but rolled back onto her feet. Anette and Fenrir counted on her. Mikael wasn't far behind her as she reached the cabin at the end of the lake, and knocked on the ogre's door.

It slid open, that wrong smile waiting

'I'm lost; can I borrow your phone?'

'Yes, come in from the cold little girl.'

'I'm not disturbing you?'

'No, just surfing the web.'

'You get Wi-Fi out here?'

'Enough to suit my needs.'

The ogre shut – and locked – the front door. Helga drew a deep breath and screamed. *Where's Mikael?* Long moments stretched like a noose around her neck. She panicked as the man lunged toward her.

The sound of smashing glass and the crackle of the radio. The glint of handcuffs in the firelight. The computer monitor flashed in the corner of the room. Helga glanced out of the window at the four scarecrows. The epiphany hit at the height of her fear.

'He's the janitor. Mikael – God! – he's the school janitor.' When Mikael had finished reading the man's rights, Helga smiled. 'I know your name now. You have no power anymore.'

Later on, after Helga had given her statement, she came home to find Fenrir by the fire, still dozy from the sedatives. Mikael stopped by on his way home to tell them that the janitor's computer had been seized and Fenrir's results would arrive within 48 hours.

She let Fenrir creep into her bed that night. He licked her face as if to say, *It wasn't me.*

Father had waffles on the grill the next morning, the radio on in the background. For once he didn't complain about the sugar when Helga downed her waffles in maple syrup. '...A man has been charged with harassment leading to the death of four teenagers…' Helga leaned over to turn up the volume. '…He allegedly lured victims to a nearby bridge after bullying them online, where they met their ends to escape his ceaseless abuse. The victims' families have described 57-year-old school-janitor Eagal Ødegård as a modern-day troll. Local officer Mikael Aasen made the arrest after...'

Father switched off the radio. 'Don't want you listening to any more, snowflake,' he said.

His eyes were warm as maple syrup, just blue. Helga sighed.

'I did know Anette actually. You never met her; before mum died you were always away working.'

He chewed his lip like she'd hurt him. She hadn't meant to. 'I'd like to tell you about Anette, if that's okay?'

Later on, Helga found a bag of dog treats on the porch, attached to a note. *Got a press conference to attend. They're treating me like an ogre-slayer at the station. Fenrir's all-clear. Guess something else killed the goats. Mikael.*

2

BEWITCHED

Narcissa walked into the woods, a gentle mist hanging from the branches like breath freezing on a looking glass, and found herself a bed of star-moss where she could arrange her limbs. The perfect white folds of her dress shifted and parted over her milky legs, stark against the green. Narcissa checked the rose-crown with her fingertips, grimacing at a stray thorn as it bit the skin.

Blood rubies rolled down her cheek – a stray tear. Perfect. She had withdrawn into her fantasy enough that when the flash came, it was unexpected. Spots formed in her vision, and Narcissa imagined that the light heralded the arrival of some divine creature, ready to abduct her to a world of endless sun.

'You look stunning!' Zeus's voice called from behind the tripod. 'They'll love it!'

Why couldn't he let her play out the scene in her mind without interrupting? A true artist would understand. Zeus – pale as her reflection, coal-coloured hair just like hers, thick-framed glasses and nimble fingers good for mounting cameras. Always ready with the compliments. He was an easy companion, but so dull. Narcissa sighed as he trundled over the fallen leaves and thrust the camera in her face. 'Wow,' she said, 'is that me? I look—'

'Bewitching,' Zeus said. 'No filter necessary. Better get this beauty on Instagram and Pinterest like yesterday. The Ophelia crowd will love it.'

She couldn't help but smile. The fans were... well, the comments. If only her stepbrother was alive to witness how his 'ugly worm' had become the songbird. 'Cissa?'

'Yes, Zeus,' she said, wishing he would only live up to his namesake a little more. 'It's wonderful.' She pulled out her smartphone from the clutch handbag she'd hidden in the ferns and checked her messages.

'Cissa,' Zeus said, glancing at the screen. 'It's getting a bit out of control, don't you think?'

'Don't look at my personal things,' she snapped. Still, he was too gawky and innocent to understand how the world worked. She'd learned younger than most perhaps, but—

'Sorry, Cissa, but I don't think the men who talk that way are *normal...*'

'And you are?'

He withered into the ferns, kneeling close beside her tree-seat. 'Just be careful,' he said. 'Please.'

'Nothing wrong with a little attention. It's a compliment.'

'Those aren't compliments, Cissa. Why do you even message them back? You're leading them on!'

'I'm not the Pied Piper.' She laughed. 'It's only a fantasy.'

Zeus's cheeks turned as red as the apples hanging across the woodland path. 'Your whole life is a fantasy, Cissa! Nothing you do is real, nothing you say is about actual life. We only ever talk about the fairy tales your stepmum read to you—'

'*Not* my stepmother, Zeus! God, don't you ever listen? It was Mummy; she read them to me before she died.'

'Fine, but you're crazy if you don't think this will bite you someday. Your followers live all over the country. What if you bump into one of them? What if they expect to live the fantasy with you, Cissa, what then?'

She couldn't listen anymore. 'You're the deluded one,' she said, ripping the camera from his hands. 'Go home.'

'I'm your ride, remember?'

'I'll make my own way.'

'Really?' said Zeus. 'That'll be a first.'

They didn't speak for a moment. He grabbed the rucksack and slunk over to the tripod, folding it under his arm. He paused by the path as if he wanted to say something, but she tilted her chin away and he left. She listened to his dying footsteps for some time, suddenly cold in her thin dress.

Narcissa plucked off her expensive heels and slung them round the handbag strap, annoyed that she hadn't stopped Zeus from taking her changing bag with him. Stubbornness always came with a price.

Fine. Whatever. She had the camera. She'd take some pictures herself, without Zeus disapproving from behind the lens. Leaves crushed between her toes as she strayed from the path, looking for the ideal set-up to take her shot. Her dress caught on a branch, but that added to the mystique. She was the artist, after all, the one who could transform the ordinary into magic. She straddled rocks and collected a bouquet of mushrooms, slipping into a faux poisoned sleep, draped over a broken tree, perfect lipstick a little smeared.

The mist muted into an amber glow, and at last Narcissa felt she'd done herself justice. Her feet iced on the walk back, numb to the inevitable scratches. Zeus hadn't messaged to ask if she'd gotten home or anything at all. She was almost proud of him for sticking to his guns for once, even if it was against her. Maybe she had overreacted slightly. The birds whistled and sang above her as she slowed, texting words of contrition.

Narcissa's scream cut the birds short.

She caught her foot on a hidden tree stump, the ground flying up to meet her.

'God! That hurt!' She gripped her ankle, wincing when she tried to move it. Her text still hadn't gone through. She tried another, asking Zeus to help her – she couldn't walk back like this – but the signal was too weak this deep in the woods. 'Guess no one's coming to save me,' she muttered.

'Miss, do you need help?'

Oh God, why did she recognise that face? The man stared at her, a bag of chestnuts overflowing in his hands. 'Erm… yes. I've hurt my foot. Do you have a phone?'

'No, Miss.'

'Great. Can you help me to the road then; I can get signal there I think, call a taxi?'

He pushed his sandy hair out of his eyes and squinted through the gloom. 'We're a bit far out. It'll take a while to arrive, and you don't look that suitably dressed for a long wait on an October evening. My cottage is just over there.' He pointed in a vague direction. 'I have a wood burner.'

'Yeah, because that solves everything.'

'What, Miss?' He walked closer, cupping his big ears.

'That sounds great,' she said. What choice did she have, really? She'd wanted a rescuer, and here he was. A stranger, sure, but there was something starkly boyish and open about his face, and her ankle was throbbing.

'I have a first aid kit too,' he said, pointing at her foot.

Narcissa paused, then sighed. 'A bandage sounds good.'

He was strong too, supporting her weight, the camera, and the sack of chestnuts. His cottage was sweet, if a little stark, and he lit the fire like he promised and put the kettle on.

'I've called a taxi. Should be an hour or so,' he said, coming back into the kitchen with the promised bandage. 'Do you want me to bind it for you?'

'No, I can do it. Thanks.'

'I'll get on with the tea, then.' He opened the cupboard, hunting for two clean mugs. Though he took his time about it. Narcissa caught the glimpse of a trio of glossy photos pinned on the inside of the cupboard, but she was sitting at the wrong angle to see the face peering out of them. A girlfriend, perhaps?

He'd sounded a little familiar too.

Zeus's warning echoed through her mind. *They live all over the country.*

As the kettle whistled on the stove, Narcissa had the dreadful suspicion that she'd spoken to a man like this on Skype. But no, he would've recognised her, said something? Then again, he hadn't even asked about the camera, or why she'd been in the woods. Come to think of it, wasn't it one of her fans who had suggested the wood as an ideal location for a photo shoot? Zeus had thought it was her idea, but Narcissa had never even heard of these woods before.

I've got to get out of here. The man placed a mug in front of her. 'Only have herbal, I'm afraid. Health kick.'

She sipped the bitter tea, desperate to thaw her insides. 'What's your name?' she asked.

He pulled out the creaky chair and sat opposite. 'You don't remember me, Miss? That's a little disappointing.'

Her heartbeat pounded in her head. God, it was hot in this stuffy little kitchen. 'No,' she said, horrified at the smallness of her voice. 'Sort of. I recognise you.'

'I should think so. I cherished our time together.'

'Who are you?'

'The first time I saw you,' he said, leaning closer, 'I couldn't stop thinking... you're a little witch, you know that? I'd never been bewitched before.'

Her stomach flipped, her vision blurring. Her breath came short and fast. 'What's in the tea? I feel weird.'

'Hallucinogens.' He stood up. 'What's the matter? I thought you'd like it. Never been happy with the real world, have you, Cissa?'

Pain shot up her leg like a firework, but she scrambled out of the chair, chucking the scalding tea in his face. He roared, flipping the table. Somehow, she ran, feral, stumbling out the back door. Why hadn't he locked it?

'You can't run from me! You never could!'

She was crying as she fled into the evening gloom, downhill towards the stream. Zeus had parked near a stream that morning, so if she followed it – yes, uphill a little – she'd find her way back.

But the man was panting close behind her, and a breath later his hands were in her hair, pulling her downward. The horrors he spoke to her were so hauntingly familiar. That voice swamped her insides no matter how hard she screamed against it. *You're not strong enough to fight me, Cissa.*

They tumbled down the bank into the stream, her thin dress clinging to her most private places, and the memories crashed down with her, of *him*, her stepbrother, all those terrifying nights. A little girl, crying for her mother, branded a liar by her replacement. She'd been accused of losing touch, and yes, it felt so much better to pretend herself away.

How was this time any different? She'd never escape him, never...

So cold. The water ran up her nose as he pressed his weight behind her, and she gasped like a fish, suffocating. A thousand days and nights marched on the bottom of the stream bed, receding back to the last happy evenings, curled up on Mum's lap, comforted by tales of valour and true love. *Whatever forest you come to, Honey, hack your way through it.*

Oh, God, yes. How she had *hacked.* Her darkest nightmare revealed itself moments before the curtain descended, the nightmare Narcissa had kept in chains at the bottom of her imaginary dungeon. Brad, sandy-haired, and strong. The fake brother, the daytime bully and the midnight demon. The first time they'd been collecting chestnuts. The last time she'd found the rock, the rusty saw in the abandoned cottage. Only one of them had returned home.

You want this, Miss. Cissa. Sister.

Yes, the man above her had been her first follower, her first stalker, the villain looming like a dark shadow over her imaginary world. Brad. Brad. Brad. How had she hidden from it for so long? How had the phantom of him drawn her back here, to die? Well, she'd survived the last time, but a part of herself had remained in that cottage.

I've come back to collect myself, Narcissa realised, screaming through the stream, and letting out the dragon Brad had impregnated her with all those years ago.

Narcissa grabbed the hand pressing her head into the stream and found it was her own. Choking, she scrambled to her feet. The ghost of Brad was nowhere to be seen. 'I'm free,' she gasped, shivering and coughing against the bank. 'I beat you, Brad.'

Zeus came tearing out of the trees. 'Where have you been? I waited for hours by the car! I just got your—'

'Zeus?'

He pulled her out of the stream, sacrificing his coat, and wrapped his arms tightly around her. 'What happened?'

The cottage mocked her through the trees. Old, crumbling.

And on fire.

What had she done?

'This wood has held me under its spell for so long,' she said. 'It's broken now.' Her phone bleeped from a nearby rock, where she had apparently left it. Zeus picked it up. 'Give it here,' she said.

'Sorry, Cissa, I was just—'

Narcissa snatched it from his hand and tossed it into the stream. 'I'm ready for the real world now, Zeus,' she smiled. 'If you don't mind, I'd like you to be my only follower from now on.'

Zeus took her arm, hesitant. Sweet. Gentle. He'd been her perfect familiar all along; she'd just been too lost in herself to see it. 'Lead the way,' he said.

3

JEWEL

They called her India, on account of her heritage. They didn't bother to remember the name of her ramshackle village in the land of heat and colour, spice, and sacred gods.

India slept on a hard mattress in the basement, huddled close to the boiler for extra warmth, her nights passing with the drips from an old pipe and the sound of footsteps upstairs. She possessed two changes of clothes: her ragged sari that had once been her mother's, and her uniform, given to her on her first day in London by her English 'aunt', the fat cow – actually *cow* was too good for the woman without a single holy bone in her body who ran the Chelsea beauty salon.

Of course, she wasn't in any way related to that horrible woman, her supposed Indian uncle, or their daughters Sadie and Carmen. They spoke to their customers like they had adopted India – under no account was she to use her real name – as if they'd taken sympathy on the poor girl from the sticks.

'India! Where the hell are you? Lazy bitch! Get up here now.' Auntie placed a heel on the top stair of the basement but India knew it was just a warning; she wouldn't come down here, not since the first night when she had slapped India about and told her the rules. It was enough just to remember the terror to speed up her fingers on her buttons.

'Coming, Auntie!' She ran, tripping on the last step because her dear aunt had failed to remove her feet in time. She caught her fall on the doorframe but she was yanked inside the kitchenette by her bad wrist. 'Ouch.'

'Ouch? What's the matter, are you ill? Too sick to work today?'

Sadie was by the kettle. She turned and handed her mum and Carmen their tea. India was not stupid enough to answer the question or ask for a drink herself. 'Maybe she shouldn't work today, Mummy. She only owes Daddy… how much again?'

'Twenty-thousand pounds.' Auntie sneered. 'She's actually managed to increase her debt since Daddy arranged for her passage here. The silly girl keeps spending money on luxuries.'

Luxuries like food and sanitary towels. India was not entitled to anything from the salon, or their seven-bedroom mansion she had to clean single-handedly every weekend. Those girls were as slobby as they were ugly. 'I am well,' she said. 'I am happy to work.'

'Good, anyone would think you didn't appreciate your position. We pay you twice as much as you earned in that slum Uncle found you in.'

'Yes, Auntie.'

'Maybe she'd prefer the pop-up shop down the street, Mummy,' Carmen said, 'the way the husbands look at her. Only yesterday Mr Jones said something pukey about her eyes. I don't see it myself.'

'Is that what you want, India? Would you prefer to sully your honour so you can never go home and find a man to take you in?'

India felt the heat behind her eyes. The only dishonour would be to let them see how their darts pierced her. 'No, Auntie. I am grateful to work here, with family.'

Sadie checked her thin hair in the mirror above the sink and barged past, jabbing her crooked finger into India's chest. 'You're not family. Don't forget.'

'Well don't loiter all day, India,' Auntie said, pointing to the cleaning cupboard. 'You left the front of house in a mess last night. You're lucky I'm even paying you today. I found hair in the driers. You know how much I hate that.'

The second Auntie and Carmen left, India opened the cupboard and quickly filled up her water bottle at the sink, returning to cram a couple of dry biscuits she had hidden behind the bleach, into her delicate mouth. Her next break would be closing time, so it was best not to drink too much water now in case she got desperate.

The salon was busy. India hung up tailored coats and handbags that cost more money than she had earned in the last six months. Hardly anyone noticed her as they gossiped with Sadie, who cut their hair, Carmen focusing on the treatments and nails. India kept the salon immaculate, but sometimes she covered her 'cousins' during their many shopping breaks so the salon didn't have to close.

There was one woman, Lily, who would strike up conversation – an elderly lady who India treated with natural deference, as she had learned to do since childhood. Lily was her only source of kind words, the only one unencumbered with smartphones or trashy magazines, the only one who asked about her background. Perhaps if India could finally figure out the code to the safe, get her passport back, maybe Lily would listen to her story, buy her a ticket home. It was worth the risk, wasn't it?

India propped her broom out of the way and crept over to Lily, inviting her to come for her hair wash. 'Is it too hot?' India said as she sprinkled the warm water over Lily's head.

'No, dear, perfect as usual.'

India smiled. They spoke to each other with their eyes – India fascinated by the cool-blue irises that always focused on her so intently. When she had finished, Lily sat up to accept the towel round her shoulders. 'Has anyone ever told you how pretty your eyes are, dear? Surely you could do better than being an assistant?

I hope I don't sound insensitive – my granddaughter tells me off but I'm too old to be PC these days – but you look like a Bollywood star. Can you act, dance?'

India blushed. 'I can sing... My father loved it when I sang to him.'

'Where is he now, dear?'

'He has sickness of the mind. He hardly remembers me.'

'Oh, I'm sorry, if there's anything I can do.'

Her heart missed a beat. 'Well, there is—'

'Mrs Wand!' Sadie came charging up the steps to the basins, brandishing her scissors. 'How's Lacey? The wedding is Saturday, right? You'll be coming in for a blowout in the morning?'

'Of course,' said Lily, 'I must look fabulous, dear. My only granddaughter is getting married.'

'No time to lose then!' Sadie stepped in front of India, forcing her back. 'Let me give you a hand.'

'It's quite alright. I prefer to go at my own pace.'

India smiled; Lily had never rejected her arm. Her smile soured when she realised she'd lost her only chance to ask for help. The rest of the day she slogged as she desperately tried to think of a plan to speak to Lily again on Saturday. Sadie and Carmen were going to the wedding – they'd known Lacey since school – perhaps if she offered to carry their handbags and drinks, they'd let her go too. But even if she got back to India, what was to stop Uncle making good on his threats and claiming her debts from her family?

'Go and get us a kebab. Hey, Earth to India?'

'Sorry, Carmen.' India took the card and scurried to the takeaway on the corner. She had tried to ask for help from the men that ran the shop the first time, and they had offered her the very job in the brothel that Auntie had threatened her with. They had known she was an Untouchable, the lowest caste of all, forever tainted by the blood of her ancestors who worked in unsavoury professions. This time she ordered chips for herself, hoping it wouldn't be obvious on Carmen's bank statement. Not that the girl bothered to check.

The chips were scalding but she swallowed them quickly before returning to the salon. Carmen brought her to the kitchen. 'You took ages. Who did you talk to?'

'No one. I had to wait.'

Carmen opened the paper and inspected the kebab. 'Did you eat any? I bet you did; that's just like you. Always taking more than you're entitled to, and Daddy says you're not to touch our food directly because you're—'

'I do not eat meat,' India said. Stupid. Carmen knew that. She would pay for talking back.

'I think you're still sick,' she said. 'Go and rest downstairs and play with your mice.'

India was too tired to argue. She retired to the basement, shoeing the little creatures out of her blankets. India was used to vermin, and at least the mice treated her with respect.

The three days without Lily in the salon toyed with her like a cat slowly unwinding a ball of string. India made sure to finish her Saturday chores before Lily arrived for her blowout, but Sadie and Carmen were quick to part her from Lily when she arrived. 'Tea, Mrs Wand?' India asked. Sadie frowned at her.

'Yes, dear.'

'I will make it for you,' Carmen said.

Lily waved her aside. 'India does it the way I like it.' She winked at her. 'Carmen makes it too strong, and Sadie makes it too weak. And your auntie puts milk in it every time!'

She caught her smile in the mirror and stifled it, but her faux cousins had spotted her. So did Lily. 'Oh there, a smile at last! Look at those teeth. I remember when I had teeth like that.'

'I'll make the tea,' India said, hurrying back to kitchen. When she returned, they were discussing wedding outfits.

Lily sipped her tea and frowned. 'What will you be wearing, India?'

'Oh, she's not invited, right?' Carmen said. 'Didn't Lacey say how big the guest list was already?'

'Yeah,' said Sadie. 'No room at the inn.'

India met Lily's eyes. She tried to invest all her longing into her look, praying Lily would hear her silent plea. 'Well,' Lily said, setting her tea on the shelf by the mirror. 'Since my Arthur died, I don't have a plus-one. And I'm getting so unsteady on my feet these days, and weddings are such long affairs…'

'Mummy would go with you,' Sadie said.

'Oh no, she won't want to be lumbered with an old woman. India and I can keep each other amused. What do you say, India?'

'I'd like to make myself useful,' she said, unable to mask the excitement in her voice.

'It's settled then.'

'But she has nothing to wear,' Carmen blurted, 'And the wedding's this afternoon!'

'Carmen, dear,' Lily said, 'you just told me about that dress you ordered online that didn't fit. The one you didn't have time to return? Show it to me.'

It was perfect. The burnt orange set off India's skin tone perfectly, the red beading pretty but modest. It wouldn't have suited Carmen's fake tan at all. 'Problem solved. I'll tell my driver to stop by on our way to the wedding.' She patted India's wrist. 'Half-twelve sharp, dear.'

'Yes, Mrs Wand.'

'Oh, and Carmen? Lend the dear some of your make-up.'

A limousine pulled up outside the salon. India's three chaperones had waited with her, and Lily was too polite not to invite them to ride along too. India sat as close to Lily as she dared but hardly said a word; every time she opened her mouth, Auntie looked at her the way she did before each beating.

The wedding, at a local church, was the first English wedding India had ever seen. It wasn't as colourful as she was used to, but the horse-drawn carriage Lacey arrived in was enough to make her heart ache with longing, and the choir singers brought tears to her eyes. India recognised some of the guests from the salon, but it was the best man that drew her attention. Other than herself, he was the only Asian face in the crowd.

He *winked* at her. He laughed with the groom, a ginger-haired rake that despite being handsome, appeared more like the man's poodle. India looked at her feet as the ceremony began. She hardly saw the bride's dress behind the broad backs of Carmen and Sadie – there hadn't been enough room at the front to sit with Lily. After the vows and the signing, the church emptied out behind Lacey and Geoff.

'India!' Lily was waiting for her next to the pew, the best man on her arm. 'You've made an impression on Harry.'

India took Lily's free arm and blushed. 'What can I say,' said Harry. India expected a witty follow-up, but none came.

'I've never known Harry to be lost for words.'

They escorted Lily outside. India avoided the photographer, but at one point she walked over to a tree and Harry appeared at her shoulder, where she was ambushed by a bright flash. Auntie was watching her so she dashed back onto the path, but then there was a shriek and India jumped, throwing her hands up by reflex, shocked to see the bride's bouquet of flowers in her grasp.

'What a waste,' Sadie sneered. Everyone was staring at her. She turned to flee, hide anywhere but under their scrutiny, but Harry was a giant roadblock on the path and she was trapped.

'Hi,' he said, 'who's the lucky man?'

'No one.'

'No one?'

'No one.'

She didn't speak to anyone again until they arrived at the venue, an old hall that reminded her of a ballroom. The scent of the flower decorations was so strong she sneezed three times into the crook of her arm.

'Handkerchief?' Harry said, pulling the one out of his jacket pocket. 'I hoped it would come in handy.'

'Thank you,' she said.

Harry sneezed into his big hands. 'You must be contagious,' he said. 'Where's a man's handkerchief when he needs one?'

India folded the handkerchief and offered it to Harry. He took it. 'Thanks, I've always had a sensitive nose. So how did you meet Lily?'

Sadie pushed in, eclipsing Harry. 'Yeah, she works for *us*. She's a distant relative of a friend of Daddy's. He's in India, looking after the family's interests.' Sadie pressed the back of her high heel into India's sparkly pumps, but luckily it slipped between her toes. 'Lily comes into the salon.'

Harry peered over Sadie's head. 'Well, you're not taking care of her. Look how skinny she is.' He pointed in the direction of the lavish buffet running along the back wall. 'I've lost my best mate to Lacey. India, keep me company?'

'I better get back to Lily.'

'We'll get her a plate too. Come on, I'm starving.' Harry reached around Sadie and held out his hand.

I will regret this, India thought, but her stomach growled, her head light and floaty from thirst. She took Harry's hand, not daring to glance over her shoulder. He held her firmly but his grip was relaxed, and he timed his footsteps with hers, though he was far taller. 'I am vegetarian,' she said as he passed her a plate.

'Me too,' he said, 'though you wouldn't know it by the size of my biceps.' He tensed his muscles under his suit, posing his arms and contorting his face into a series of ridiculous expressions.

India maintained her composure, raising an eyebrow. 'Wow, tough crowd.' Harry smiled.

'I'm laughing inside,' she said.

'Fine. Give me something to work on. By the end of the evening—'

'I'm a Dalit, we're Untouchable,' she blurted, as he placed a samosa on her plate. 'Sorry, I think you should know.'

He stared at her blankly. 'Oh,' he said, 'I was born in Chelsea, you know. So were my parents. We don't adhere to that stuff in my family.'

India sucked in a deep breath. She picked up two slices of French bread and put one next to his samosa. They spoke no more about it; in fact, Lily did most of the talking when they joined her at the table. Harry poured India some orange juice after she refused the champagne, keeping his eyes on her throughout the meal.

Sadie and Carmen made several attempts to draw her away, but Lily clutched her arm tightly each time they strayed near. The band set up and the tables were pushed aside to extend the dance floor.

'Harry!' Carmen kissed him on both cheeks. 'Dance with me!'

'And me,' Sadie said.

'How's a man to choose?' Harry smiled, turning to India. She turned away from him. Embarrassing her cousins, by dancing with Harry before they did, was dangerous. It only took one call to their father in India and her family... 'Well, I guess it's first come, first served.' He took Carmen's hand and twirled her around the dance floor.

It was time. Time to tell Lily what was going on, ask for her to make enquiries about her family. Harry would have contacts in India still, she was sure. You didn't just take off your cultural heritage like a suit. Lily was still at the table – alone, watching the bridesmaids pick their dance partners.

'Where do you think you're going?' Sadie dug her nails into India's arm. 'I've been watching you. I know what you're up to.'

India's stomach felt like a volcano. 'I—'

'You think Harry likes you? That you're seducing him? You're an easy lay, that's all. A man like him can smell a virgin like you a mile away.'

Suddenly India was spun around and found herself in the middle of the dance floor with Harry. 'Are you okay? Why do I get the impression you don't like Carmen and Sadie?' He lightly rested his hand on her lower back as they swayed side to side.

'It's more they don't like me,' she said.

He lowered his head and whispered in her ear. 'They're jealous, Jewel.'

'What?' She twisted under his arm, ignoring that last word.

'Because...' Harry said, '... sure, they have money, but they're cardboard cut-outs. Imitations of the real thing.'

'Huh?'

They moved in time with the music. 'Do I have to spell it out?' He gestured the length of her body. 'I have never seen such a beauty in all my life.'

'There is more to a woman than her beauty.'

He laughed. 'I agree. Carmen and Sadie are sorely lacking in that department also. They know less about England than my grandparents did when they emigrated.'

India giggled. 'See, told you I'd make you laugh.'

'They are clever enough to hurt me,' she said, and just then the music stopped.

'What do you mean, Jewel?'

The music started again. Now it was her auntie's hand on her shoulder, pulling her away. Harry was left behind, lost in a sea of grinding bodies. Sadie dragged him back into the melee. India frantically tried to spot Lily, but her escort had disappeared. She was forced to sit with Auntie and a table of strangers, hoping Harry would come back for her.

He was a popular dance partner.

'What is that mad bat doing on the stage?' Auntie said.

India looked up. Lily was hauling the microphone away from the singer. The instruments slowly petered out. 'Good evening, my dears,' she said. 'The bride and groom are keen to start the karaoke!'

The huge hall echoed with a mixture of groans and cheers. 'India? Where are you, dear? The one who catches the bride's bouquet must be the first to sing! It's a family tradition.'

India stood up slowly, the crowd on the dance floor parting to let her through. She couldn't believe it, but she couldn't disappoint Lily at her granddaughter's wedding. It would be dishonourable.

Harry was standing next to the stage, and he started the slow clap that ushered her up the steps. 'I don't know any English songs,' she whispered to Lily.

'This beautiful young lady is going to sing a traditional Indian love song,' Lily said into the microphone. India shook as she took Lily's place. The clapping stopped. Her throat constricted. Sadie and Carmen wore the glow of hatred. She couldn't do this, she just couldn't.

Harry walked up the steps, meeting her eyes with a kind of solemn amusement, and sat at the piano at the side of the stage. A delicate harmony of notes filled the hall. India felt her shoulders soften. She closed her eyes and imagined she was by her father's bedside, singing of Krishna and Radha, the heavenly counterpart to her parent's love. Her voice quivered at first but soon found its fullness, Harry keeping perfect time beside her. It was the most exhilarating experience.

The tears prickled; Lacey and her new husband had taken to the dance floor for the first time as if they had been waiting for her voice to set their feet alight. As the notes tapered off, the clapping began again, and India took Harry's arm and walked with him back into the party.

'You are amazing,' Harry said.

'As are you.'

'Nimble fingers,' he said, wiggling them. Sadie and Carmen were fast approaching. 'Hey, what did you mean about them being clever enough to hurt you?'

Maybe it was the panic or the emotion of the song. 'The man who calls himself my uncle paid for me to come to England,' she said, slipping with him deeper into the crowd. 'Now I owe him a great debt and I cannot repay him, but I can't leave Auntie until I do.'

'But you're working in the salon?' He had to shout over the music.

'I earn less than five pounds a day.'

He opened his mouth but paused, then frowned. His big hand patted her shoulder mechanically. 'How much do you owe?'

'Twenty thousand.'

'This isn't right, India. It isn't legal.'

Carmen squeezed through a dancing couple and charged over to them. 'Let's dance,' Harry said, yanking her around. He stood on her toes twice, busy avoiding Carmen and Sadie.

'It isn't legal to be in this country,' she said. 'I realised Uncle had lied the moment I arrived. If I don't pay my debt, my father and mother will be hurt.'

Harry loosened his tie with one hand. 'This isn't what I expected when I woke up this morning. Does Lily know about this?'

'No.'

India's luck ran out. They twirled right into Auntie, backed up by her daughters. In that moment, Lacey jumped in, demanding the dance from Harry. It happened so quick, and the only person who knew the truth and seemed to care was gone.

'Let go, you're hurting me,' India cried, as she was dragged out into the foyer. A taxi was waiting outside at the bottom of the steps. They forced her outside, into the taxi. It was only when they were halfway down the street that India realised she had lost one of her glittery pumps.

This time, they didn't return to the salon, but the mansion.

'You have proven yourself untrustworthy,' Auntie said. 'I should've left you in the basement. What did you say to Harry? Don't you dare lie to me!' She pressed her nails into India's thigh.

'Please,' India said, 'I did nothing.'

If she told that woman the truth, she'd never leave the mansion again. The taxi driver ignored her cries while India was interrogated in the back seat, and turned his head as Sadie held her by the hair and took her into the cold entrance hall. She closed her eyes and heard Harry playing the piano in her mind, listened to herself sing an endless internal refrain as nails and fists clawed and hammered into her. After some minutes, she heard nothing, tasting only blood in her mouth. In the darkness, she was led to her dungeon. 'Your uncle will be angry,' Auntie said, the only thing she had said since closing the big front door behind her. Now she shut the door on India's tiny prison, a lock clicking into place.

India shivered, slid down the wall, and lived nightmares with her head between her knees.

A strip of light penetrated the room, revealing that she was underground. India's joints clicked and creaked from the cold and she stumbled over to the tiny half-window, straining her neck to see what lay outside. Dirt was smeared over the window, a little grass beyond. It was possible she was beneath the kitchen, which meant she might be looking out towards the driveway. But she'd never been down here.

The door wouldn't budge.

Footsteps. India held her breath and listened. Voices arguing, muffled. Cupping her hand against the door made little difference. Then the voices came closer. India stepped back.

'Well, what are we meant to do? Pretend she never worked for us?' Carmen.

'Don't be stupid. Lily—'

'She can't stay here. Mummy already had to open the salon. On a Sunday! Of course, they didn't find anything.'

'What if they're watching the house? If we move her and they catch us…'

'I told Mummy, we should've finished the job off last night.'

Silence. India clutched her stomach. 'Mummy's told the police India went to the airport last night. She'll arrange something while they're looking – send her to Manchester or somewhere. Perhaps she'll be happier on her back all day, pleasing those men that seem to find her so irresistible.'

No! I'd rather die!

From the window, India heard the sound of tyres on gravel. So she *was* near the driveway. Carmen and Sadie were arguing loud enough that they didn't hear India creeping to the back of the room to move an old crate to the window. She climbed up and pressed her face against the glass. Auntie's car. She was alone. No police had come back with her to look for India.

The police had no reason to care about a girl lost in the cracks. But the absence of Lily and Harry stabbed her through the heart. How long would it take for Auntie to transfer her? It must've been mid-morning already. She'd want her gone by nightfall, five o'clock if she was lucky.

Lucky. She had never been lucky.

'Girls!'

'Coming, Mummy!'

India placed her hands on her knees and retched. Her fingertips were blue. She searched her prison – it must've been a storage room – and found a moth-eaten jumper that was far too small for any of the women upstairs, and a blanket that matched the one on her bed at the salon. *What if,* India thought, *what if these belonged to another girl, one before me?* What had become of her?

Was she destined to follow in her footsteps?

The faint ring of the house phone. India pressed her forehead against the wall. When she opened her eyes, the room had darkened, as if she had passed out and awoken to the night.

She heard a sneeze. India whipped round to face the window. Harry's nose was pressed into the grass. He sneezed again. 'Harry?' India climbed on the crate and wrapped her knuckles on the glass.

'India!'

He waved her back, sat up, and pointed at the window. India grabbed the blanket and placed it on the upturned crate. Harry put his boot through it, and the blanket caught the shattered glass, masking some of the noise. 'Are you okay? Your cheek—' She folded the blanket and chucked it in the corner.

Her hands flew to her face. 'Please get me out of here,' she said, 'and what are you doing crawling on the front lawn?'

'Looking for you! I couldn't believe the police bought their story. I'm not exactly meant to be here.' He pulled her lost pump from his coat pocket. 'Here, you left this behind. You might need it. Get ready to run.'

'Hurry! I think I hear someone coming. Auntie wants to get rid of me.'

Harry reached through the window and touched her hair. He scrambled out of sight just as someone put the key in the door. India put her pumps on, located an old rag and used it to pick up a piece of jagged glass. She meant it; she would rather die than be anyone's prostitute.

Auntie stepped into the dank, little room. 'Well, I see you've made yourself at home.' She looked at the window. 'How did you do that?'

'It was already broken,' India lied.

'You tried to escape. You failed.'

'I'm not going with you,' India said.

'What's in your hand?'

'Would you like to find out? Come closer.'

Auntie hesitated. 'You're lining your own coffin,' she said. 'And your family's. Just how many siblings do you have? Your lot could never keep their legs closed. You'll enjoy your new profession.'

'How can you say this?' India hissed. 'Are you not a woman? You have daughters! How can you assign me to such a fate?'

Auntie laughed. 'I haven't treated you any worse than your own society treats you. You should thank me for the opportunity to serve your betters.' She lunged forward, catching India off guard and dragging her to her knees by her hair. 'There's a good girl. Come quietly and your family will be safe.' Auntie reached for her wrist, trying to wrangle India's weapon from her fingers. India sliced at her ear.

Auntie screamed and clamped her hand to the side of her head, the blood oozing through her fingers.

'Sadie! Carmen!' She kicked India in the stomach. 'Bring the chains! And the rifle!'

India jumped to her feet and ran down the corridor and up the stairs beyond the door, holding her weapon out in front of her. She didn't notice the chain held taut at the top of the stairs. She fell, hating the world as she turned on to her back, the cool end of the rifle pressed against her forehead.

'Move, and I'll blow it off,' Carmen spat.

Auntie stormed up the stairs. 'Chain her up, quickly.' Sadie bent down to carry out the order. India screamed with every lung fibre she had ever used to sing with, kicking her legs and landing a foot on Auntie's face. Carmen caught her arm before she fell back down the stairs.

The blood drained from their faces. 'What's that?'

Auntie balled her fists. 'Sirens.'

Three sets of hands came for her, dragging her to her feet. She felt the gun in her back as Sadie pushed her forward. Men were shouting from the driveway, banging against the front door.

'Ahem.'

The pressure against her back released. India twisted in

Carmen's arms and saw Harry standing there, rifle in hand, Sadie unconscious at his feet. 'Let. Her. Go.'

Carmen shoved India to the floor and ran out of the room, Auntie following – straight into the arms of the waiting officers. 'In there,' Auntie wailed, 'That man has broken into our house and assaulted us!'

Harry dropped the rifle and held up his hands. 'I'm the one who called it in!' he shouted. 'They are keeping this woman prisoner!'

'That's a lie!'

'Your husband has just been apprehended,' the officer said, 'for offences relating to people trafficking and slavery. He's being deported back to England as we speak.'

'But that's impossible,' Auntie said, 'I only called him—'

'Mrs Khatri, I am arresting you on suspicion of holding a person in slavery or servitude, and requiring a person to perform forced or compulsory labour. You do not have to say anything—'

A policewoman entered the sitting room where India and Harry were frozen. Sadie was stirring at their feet. 'India? My name is Denise.' The woman held out her hand. 'Please, come with me. You're safe, love.' Another officer came in and dealt with Sadie and another face appeared to talk to Harry but try as they might, she wouldn't let go of his hand.

'They have my passport,' India said. 'I need it back. I need to go home.'

'Don't worry, love,' Denise said, 'we'll find it.' She led India and Harry to one of the police cars.

'Where are we going?'

'We need to ask you some questions at the station, but then we can take you to a safe house.'

'She can stay with me,' Harry said.

Denise opened the side door. 'It's a little risky,' she said, 'until we can be sure what's been going on here.'

'I just want to go home,' India said, wiping her eyes.

'Not alone, surely?' Harry squeezed her hand. 'Is that safe?' Before Denise could reply, he added, 'I'll come with you.'

'I cannot bring a strange man back to my family!' India climbed into the car. 'They must be so ashamed already.'

Harry walked round to the other side and got in. 'What if…' he said, cracking his knuckles. 'What if I went as your fiancé?'

She stared at him for a long moment. 'We live in a slum.'

Harry shrugged. 'As did my grandparents.' He smiled. 'For years, I've been looking for a jewel in the rough. What do you think?'

'I think,' she said as Denise got into the driver's seat, 'it's my choice.' Harry frowned, uncertain. She hooked her little finger around his, bridging the gap between them. 'I've chosen, Harry.'

4

MATCHSTICK GIRLS

We met on Westminster bridge. The air froze in our lungs, our lips were tinged blue, but we had both come to witness the frosting of the Thames. I think perhaps we were more desperate to forget the hidden world we inhabited.

You had a bruise smeared across your cheek, but I did not pry. Street women like us shared nods and eyebrow raises and shrugs, talking in answers instead of questions. We all had a shared history.

But you were new in town, so I took you on the grand tour around the Houses of Parliament, Big Ben, the works. And the places ostracised from the tourist map: the best bins with food still sealed, the public toilets, the begging spots where you could spend a few hours before being moved on.

I guess I shouldn't have been surprised that a girl with a posh name like Emily, with the queen's own accent, wrinkled her nose at the half-eaten baguette I offered her after finding it discarded in St James' Park. In the end, Emily, you gave in. We sat close, huddling against the cold, but even then, I sensed there was more between us than the superficial need for survival. For some reason, I starting talking about periods, where to get rags, about the kind old lady who'd wait outside the corner shop the last day of each month with a box of tampons for me.

Your face said it all – you hadn't even thought about it, had you? You were just too busy running from him, and when you took off your gloves to show me the engagement ring, your hands trembled – the shake of addiction – and that was why the shelter hadn't taken you in. They weren't equipped for the ones who damaged themselves.

It took you one day, Emily, to pawn that ring to buy that liquor and get your fix. I accepted a few sips because my bones felt like they would crack like melting ice sheets if I didn't. When you cried and smashed the last empty bottle on the floor, I took you back to my tent, do you remember that? How we held each other and spoke as new lovers, sharing nothing but broken dreams and desperation. There was nothing I could do to take away your memories, but after that long night, you were smiling through your tears. Luckily, the soup kitchen was open, and I found myself introducing you to the other women as my girlfriend. Your eyes darted around. They took you as shy, but I knew what you were searching for when you licked your lips like that. The stronger stuff wasn't on the menu here.

You were so sick. The high-born lady turned into a madwoman in rags. Love makes you do crazy things. That's what they say, isn't it? Love, in my case, helped you to shoplift and steal from tourists who didn't have the sense to secure their rucksacks and back pockets. I tried to keep you away from the harder stuff, but as the weeks passed, the gaps in your story became more apparent, and all the funny tales and witty quips could only paper those cracks.

You left me, Emily, for the man on the estate. He'd give you things with a smile that I had tried to shield you from. Hearing you unzip the tent and slip away in the middle of the night – you took my oxygen with you, the betrayal leaving me a gasping wreck until sunrise. Having prepared my tirade, I'd wait, sitting in my sleeping bag. But every morning you returned, I ended up thanking heaven you'd come back at all, when so many had fallen before you, leaving shadows on my heart.

A few days before Christmas, Emily, you vanished altogether. On Christmas Eve, I found you on Westminster Bridge, face swollen and bruised. You promised you'd never visit that man again, and I believed you – I wished so hard, and it almost seemed attainable over the roast dinner at the shelter on Christmas Day, the presents we received from perfect strangers, so they could absolve their consciences for another year.

We even watched the New Year fireworks over the Thames, laughing and clapping like everyone else in the crowd. Amongst those bodies, we were the warmest we had been in months.

We relieved the revellers of a fair chunk of change too. The next day, you revealed your resolution: invest in some smuggled cigarettes, sell them on. It wasn't what I'd envisioned, but I was cold, hungry, tired, and your eyes burned the sun's secret fuel.

They dubbed us The Matchstick Girls. We sold as many matches and lighters as we did smokes. I never asked what you spent your money on, but I saved as much as possible, burying it all over Westminster. Remember, Emily, when you asked why I carried that old map with me, the one I bought from Oxfam? I changed the subject. Why are you smoking our supplies? You know what's in that crap? And you had said that you didn't know — and it didn't matter anyway, like somehow you had known what was coming.

The snow came. I dug up some of the change so we could ride the bus and keep out the cold. You got some more customers that way; in fact, it was around then you told me about those business classes you had taken before you'd gotten engaged. To think I had sheltered you under my wing, but now you could match names to faces all over London. I started learning from you, and sometimes things became very dark, sometimes we only just escaped.

The street dealers tolerated us until they didn't, until the men they answered to deigned to take us seriously. Emily, I warned you, but you didn't listen, and suddenly we were cutting into their bottom line, and that only stoked your fire harder, and you moved so fast all the time, you stopped talking about the snow and pain in your hands.

We moved around a lot. Wasn't a good idea to stay in the same spot, you said, though no one had bothered me in my little, hidden nook before. You started carrying a big old kitchen knife in your puffer coat, and that's when I really started getting scared. There was no way we could stay in Westminster; either the gangs would exterminate us on the streets or in jail. I applied for us to relocate to the West Country – I had an aunt there, though I hadn't met her as an adult, and the council would pay for our ticket.

But you wouldn't go. That's when I finally understood; my Emily was on a one-woman vengeance quest.

Because the fiancé you'd abandoned, he'd broken you as he had so many others, supplied you with your own destruction as he supplied Westminster. He had been hunting you, and that was why we used decoys, ever-changing passwords and trading points, all of it. You had been in control of this since I met you on that bridge.

But the tide catches up with everyone, Emily.

I had never seen you so scared as before the big meeting. You'd groomed the contacts for months, made attachments, uncovered weaknesses. Admit it, you were cocky, weren't you? Until the moment you turned on me and told me I had to stay behind in the tent, just in case. Your hands were shaking again, but not because of the booze. This was different. I silently crouched and zipped up the tent, walking past you toward the street.

And then I fell – you struck me from behind – and I awoke in the pitch-dark tent, scrambling outside with sirens screeching in my head. I'd never learned to coordinate my limbs when I ran, but that night I could have destroyed Paula Radcliffe on my own marathon.

Deep within my stomach, I could feel it. I was running for your life, Emily. My trainers pounding the pavement, my head clearing despite the panic. Without your constant reassurance, I saw the chain of events linking in the air before me like street lights blinking on, forming a spider's web across the City. Emily, oh Emily, I think you knew too. Who was behind it, drip-feeding you the information, luring you to your fate.

I came to the rendezvous but of course I was too late. That old, boarded-up restaurant was empty, other than the shattered glass and the blood. My guts foamed to the surface and I heaved up all the lies you must've told me, but in that instant I forgave you.

It was dawn when your body was found, tethered near our bridge. You were meant as a message. Yours was not a death to be hidden. I don't recall how long I screamed for. I saw nothing but the face that was and wasn't yours for days afterward, huddled alone in the tent. It was always night and I always shivered.

Now I feel nothing, Emily. I am in the tent but there's no boundary to it anymore. Birdsong. I hear it. Wood pigeon and something else. I strain my ears and swear I can pick out crickets far away. Humming, like a dragonfly. I think the night is ending. I reach up but my limbs don't move, and my whole self is missing. But we were always so light and skinny, I suppose. The Matchstick Girls. Skinny as a cigarette.

I hear the zip. The tent is opening and the light floods in so bright that the face peering down at me is a silhouette. A hand reaches in, takes mine, the feeling suddenly flooding back into my fingertips. I am strong. I step outside.

A train door closes behind me. Someone is blowing a whistle. The scene takes moments to settle, like one's balance readjusting to land after a trip on the water.

Strands of caramel-blond hair blow in front of my eyes, obscuring the sign affixed to the wall. I can't quite make out the letters, Emily, but I think it's you here with me, at a station in the West Country. We must have caught that train, after all. Your arms circle my neck and it's as if you've unzipped my coat and stepped right inside it with me. 'Is my aunt picking us up?' I ask.

'No, she's not here yet.' We walk arm-in-arm into the station-house, and the room is crowded. A man, neat beard and glossy hair, weaves effortlessly around the bodies. He nods and points to the tickets we're holding in our hands.

He punches two holes but pockets the tickets. 'Follow me,' he says, and his voice seeps like treacle into my mind. 'I'll give you the grand tour.'

We hesitate. He holds out his hands, and they draw us like magnets to his side. He smells like lavender and honey and toffee. 'Don't worry,' he says, 'you're going to love it here.'

I believe him, Emily. I think by your smile that you do too.

5

WAKE

Massive head injury; I'm afraid your daughter is in a comatose state.

Gwen tried to tell her mum that it was alright. She shouted into the darkness, but her voice boomed back, trapped. Mum's perfume filled this inner place, and suddenly this cave Gwen inhabited filled with waves of that scent, running up what she took to be her nose, until she was forced to breathe it in.

She's breathing on her own. That's a good sign, isn't it, Doctor...?

Doctor Jenkins. But you can call me Sam. It's encouraging.

A draught of air wafted over Gwen's limbs. She felt herself tumbling down the side of a snowy mountain, but when she hit the bottom she heard the click of a door rather than a thud.

This is Doctor Fay Turner, Gwen's consultant.

I'm sorry we're meeting under these circumstances.

I was just asking Sam, I mean Doctor Jenkins, about Gwen breathing on her own. That's good, right?

Yes, but her brain suffered a lot of trauma in the car accident. Her condition could worsen.

Sam?

I'll do everything I can to make Gwen comfortable.

Crying. Gwen was running down an endless corridor, searching every room for Mum. Each door opened to the bare hospital room, Mum's soft sobbing moving ever farther away like a hunted rainbow. The floor became sticky, slowing her progress, and soon she was crawling, her hands sinking into the wooden surface and holding her fast. The more effort Gwen deployed to escape, the deeper she sank. Apathy gained its stranglehold, the time of her imprisonment stretching slowly, like the viscous glue cocooning her. It took her an age to turn onto her back.

The roof of the corridor faded away, and she saw atom bombs, stars exploding, and felt it all inside her skull. The blinding light, the polluting ash, the terrible pressure behind her eyes.

Swelling, pressing down on her brain stem.

When will she wake up?

It's impossible to say for sure. She's in the best care.

The goo holding Gwen in place slackened, and arms condensed around her, drawing her in for a hug. *I'm in the best care.* The rich, masculine voice that had penetrated her fugue was nothing like the clipped, clinical tones of the other, female voice.

Gwen licked her lips. Cotton buds tumbled from her tongue, floating around her. The air tasted like cardboard, and it was as if she'd been licking an iron bar, if her mouth was anything to go by. She attempted to speak. *Sam. I like that name.*

Just cotton buds.

What music does she like? There's an MP3 dock in the corner.

She likes Metallica...

A girl after my own heart, Mrs. Arch.

Miss Arch.

Sorry. I can bring something in for Gwen, if it's easier, Miss Arch. We apparently share the same taste.

Thanks, I can't think about MP3s and playlists right now. Call me Jessica.

No problem, we'll be rocking in here all night.

The pressure behind Gwen's eyes migrated to her chest. The

amber glue was replaced with a pile of heavy rocks, covering every inch of her body except her nose. Buried alive. She recalled that scene from Kill Bill, where whoever it was escaped from a coffin buried underground by punching through the lid. It would be a stretch to say Gwen's hand was the same as the image of punching she held and watched play out, but eventually, she wriggled to the surface of her rock pile, and the muffled garble she'd heard down below sharpened.

I like this one, Gwen. Wherever I May Roam, orchestral version. It seems right. Where are you now, Gwen? What can you see? What can you hear?

I hear you, Sam.

The surgery went as well as can be expected. Mum will be back later with some of your things. You're not alone, I promise. No man – or woman – is an island on my watch.

Gwen peered out from her mound of rocks. They shifted in time with the musical beats, and palm trees spouted from saplings to adults, heavy with coconuts. She wriggled her toes into the warm sand below her. A strip of blue glistened in the near distance. The breeze carried the scent of pineapple and salt. God, the thirst. Maybe she could find a stream with clean water. The rocks slid away, and she followed their descent onto the beach, a perfect huskless coconut falling into her waiting hands, the three holes on the top of the outer shell already open. She sipped the sweet milk, her sore throat softening like hot wax.

Your drip is a little low, Gwen. I'll change it for you now. Don't want you getting dehydrated.

A wave of relief spread over her. The coconut was gone, lost in the cascading waterfall pouring over her head.

The nurse will be here soon; I'll make sure she freshens you up a bit before Mum gets back.

A face peered through the waterfall. A man's face. A kind face, with downy, neat hair decorating the chin and upper lip. The mouth moved in time with the words that echoed over the falls, and Gwen laughed with the blessing of company. She'd never minded being alone; sure, she worked hard at university, she raced her bike on weekends. But fastened inside herself, this strange yet familiar face was a joy to behold.

Thank you for coming, Sam.

As soon as the face appeared, it drew back through the curtain of water and left her cold and stranded.

Mum came and went, holding her hand and talking about the news and latest gossip, and Gwen tried to surface on those occasions to enjoy it, but the forest standing between her and consciousness grew thick and lush, a million vines entangling every footstep. Occasionally she'd pass a wrecked car, a sleek motorbike, some treasured item from her past, and phantoms of her future. A mountain rose up in the distance, its snowcap blushing pink like the underbelly of a conch.

Doctor Turner says you're getting worse. I can't lose you, Gwen. I can't lose my daughter. Please, come back to us.

We've got some cards to read to you. Sam. Gwen looked past the canopy of her forest and spotted a bright star that illuminated the path ahead. Sam's caramel voice floated down on the beams of light. Holding out her palms, she absorbed the flakes of well-wishes from her family and friends as he read them out.

Gwen leant forward, attacking the vines with a sharp rock, powering herself uphill. At last, progress. If only Sam could stay all the time, whispering in her ear. Mum helped too, but the pain and desperation in her tone scared Gwen as much as it comforted her. She understood she was sick, that something was terribly wrong with her mind, that this world and this epic trek wasn't her normal life, but it had reality nonetheless, and it was the most important quest she'd ever undertaken. Winning against this forest was the difference between life and death. Just as when she dreamed, Gwen sensed things about her environment that weren't immediately obvious to her senses. She wanted to share her struggle with Mum and Sam, tell them that she was fighting as hard as she could, but words failed her as much as her feet did.

She needed them to be the sword in her hand. *I will win this.* Doctor Turner, that hard, rational devil on her shoulder, believed the opposite was likely.

Gwen had always had trouble with authority figures.

It's been three weeks with no progress. It's time to consider the possibility that she might not wake up, Doctor Jenkins.

We shouldn't talk about this in front of her.

Miss Arch is coming. I'm just asking you not to give her false hope.

Fay, you know as well as I do that things can change rapidly and at any time.

Exactly, Sam, but not always in the direction we hoped. I'm just being pragmatic.

Jessica! Hi!

Three weeks? Was that right? Three months? Three years? How old was she? When was her birthday? What month was it? Where did she live? Gwen realised these were the first rational questions she had asked herself in, well, however long she'd been here.

There was a castle on her mountain now. The left turret was crumbling, the gatehouse forlorn. It was still some distance away, but in rare moments, her vision could span the gulf to the extent that she could touch the rough stone with her sight alone.

Gwen's head swayed heavily on her shoulders. She shook the weight off, surprised when a jewel-studded headdress landed at her feet. The heat of the forest was making it difficult to breathe, difficult to understand what she was seeing. She tugged at her ragged shirt, her fingers finding instead a whalebone corset – leashed tight at her back – the top half of a turquoise dress that skirted her ankles. So, she was a princess, was she? Lost from her castle? That didn't fit with the image of the woman that tapped in the background as incessantly as the woodpeckers she often came across. There was no prince hacking through the forest to find her. This was a mission for her alone. She didn't need rescue, she just needed to…

She needed to…

Wake up, Gwen. Please, open your eyes. Move your fingers. Anything. I'm not ready to give up hope.

The ground shook beneath her feet, a tremor that spread across the forest floor. Gwen dived to the nearest tree, clinging on to the unforgiving trunk she encircled with her nails.

Jessica, shaking her won't help. Here, I brought some coffee. Why don't you tell me more about her? You told me yesterday she's got a Harley Davidson. I bet you were worried the first time she rode off on that, right?

Terrified. Thanks for the coffee.

And she came back, didn't she?

She hit a tree, actually. But yeah, she came back – in a cast.

Did that stop her?

No...

Then you've got to trust she's strong enough to find her way back to us. I mean, back to you.

Sam, she's beautiful, isn't she? I know you can't say, but I—

Doctor Turner? Any news?

The swelling has eased slightly, Miss Arch. But not as much as we hoped.

Gwen steadied herself against the tree and started walking. The castle was getting closer, but it was disintegrating with each sunrise and sunset. Time was trickling down the hill and churning the path behind her to mud. There was no going back. The castle had to be reached; it had to be saved.

Fay, her finger twitched twice last night.

Sam, I've noticed you're getting attached to Gwen. I've seen it happen before. No, I'm not saying you're wrong.

Gwen measured time by bursts of lucidity, by the number of hands that tapped her veins and moved her around the bed. In these moments, her consciousness hovered at the front of her mind, delicate as China crockery, liable to topple and smash at a breath's notice.

Morning, Gwen. I thought I'd read you a story. Your mum said it was your favourite as a child. Once upon a time, there was a spiteful and mean-hearted fairy who hated the King and Queen. When they had a child, after failing to conceive for many years, the royal house threw an enormous party...

Gwen paused in her flight through the trees, listening to the candy-sweet wind carrying trumpet blasts and laughter, guided by the fluttering leaves.

But the spiteful fairy wasn't invited, so she decided to curse the new child.

A dark streak blasted through the trees, leaving a blackened smear on them, seeping like ink into every crevice. The forest started to melt around her. Gwen ran.

When the princess was fully grown, she pricked her finger on an old spinning wheel she found in one of the towers of her castle and fell into a deep sleep. The courtiers and attendants told the King and Queen that their daughter was dead, but they refused to believe it. They had her carried to her bed, where she was watched over day and night, out of sight of the others. The kingdom mourned. Many years passed, and eventually the King and Queen, who never had more children, died. Their hidden princess was forgotten about, and the castle abandoned. It began to crumble

Gwen watched, helpless, as the castle on the mountain lost its left turret. The stone tumbled down the mountain, the noise echoing in the valley below her. *No! No!*

But the legend of the princess remained. In a neighbouring kingdom, the second son of a noble family left his home at daybreak to find his own riches that lay beyond the borders. Of course, many others had tried to hack through the briar forest that had grown around the abandoned castle, in search of treasure and the lost princess, but all had failed, ensnared by the thorns.

Gwen stumbled, falling to the moist earth. Her wrists and ankles were bound in wooden string.

But it just so happened that the old, cruel fairy had finally died herself. When the young prince arrived at the forest edge, the vines, trees, and bushes had blossomed with roses and wildflowers. And when he held up his heavy sword, the once impenetrable forest parted before him.

The vines unwound from Gwen's wrists, and as she sat up, the blackened trees returned to spring, blooms the size of her head sprouting in two great walls that flanked the path, which now ran unobstructed to the top of the mountain.

Gwen laughed, jumping and skipping over the pools of sunlight that led her to the castle. She was so much closer than she'd realised.

When the prince reached the castle, he was astonished by the riches he found within the crumbling walls. Paintings by the great masters, covered in thick dust. Tapestries of spun gold and silver, but most precious of all, the sleeping princess hidden at the top of the farthest turret. He thought of the ways the land had changed in the hundred years she had been cursed, and of the many wars and lives that had been lost. But her story was the most tragic of all, for she was destined to wake to discover all her loved ones and faithful subjects had long since perished in the winds of time.

Moved by her tragedy, the young prince approached her bed, determined that the beautiful young woman slumbering there would not have to navigate this new world of trials alone. The prince knelt by her pillow and took her hand in his. Her lips parted, and her eyelids fluttered, but she did not quite stir.

The prince wanted to kiss her, but he knew it was not right to touch his lips to hers until she willed it. Thus, he kissed her forehead instead.

And then she opened her eyes.

GUESS WHAT?

You have a lot of power as a reader to influence authors by leaving reviews of their work on Amazon. Reviews help authors to find the right readers too, and that makes everyone happy. So if you enjoyed these stories, please do leave a review. I read every single one, and they help me to keep producing more for my fans.

Oh, and don't forget to pick up your free chapters from my Norse Fantasy Trilogy here: BookHip.com/LVXFXB

ABOUT THE AUTHOR AND GIVEAWAY GROUP

S. A. Ashdown is an emerging author of fantasy fiction. This is her first collection of short stories.

To find out more about her work visit
www.theinkyfeather.com

For your chance to win prizes like free paperback books bundles, signed editions, and more, join the Brooker Press Giveaway group:
https://www.facebook.com/groups/brookerpress/

Printed in Great Britain
by Amazon